Out and About with the Big Tree Gang

Jo Ellen Bogart
Jill Bogart

with illustrations by
Dean Griffiths

ORCA BOOK PUBLISHERS

Library and Archives Canada Cataloguing in Publication

Bogart, Jo Ellen, 1945-

Out and about with the big tree gang / Jo Ellen Bogart, Jill Bogart;

with illustrations by Dean Griffiths.

(Orca echoes)

ISBN 1-55143-603-5

I. Bogart, Jill II. Griffiths, Dean, 1967- III. Title. IV. Series.

PS8553.O465O98 2006   jC813'.54   C2006-903097-9

First Published in the United States: 2006
Library of Congress Control Number: 2006927084

Summary: Reg, Keely, Burt and Shawna of *The Big Tree Gang* are
back for fall and winter adventures.

Orca Book Publishers gratefully acknowledges the support for its publishing programs provided by the
following agencies: the Government of Canada through the Book Publishing Industry Development
Program and the Canada Council for the Arts, and the Province of British Columbia through the
BC Arts Council and the Book Publishing Tax Credit.

Design and typesetting by Doug McCaffry

Illustrated by Dean Griffiths

Orca Book Publishers
PO Box 5626 Stn. B
Victoria, BC Canada
V8R 6S4

Orca Book Publishers
PO Box 468
Custer, WA USA
98240-0468

www.orcabook.com

Printed and bound in Canada
Printed on recycled paper, 60% PCW.
09 08 07 06 • 4 3 2 1

To my daughter and co-author, Jill, and her family.
Jo Ellen Bogart

For Patrick
Jill Bogart

The Compass

"Where's Reg?" asked Burt, when Keely arrived at Big Tree without her brother.

"He's having a talk with Dad, but he'll be along soon," Keely answered. "What's up with you guys?"

"Oh, we were just looking at the clouds," said Shawna. "That one looks like a fish, don't you think?"

"Well, it could be longer at the back, if you ask me," Keely said. She sang:

"Cloud fishy, your top fin's a sail.

I think what you need is a much bigger tail."

"I could tell you a big fish tale!" said Burt, chuckling.

5

"Hey, guys!" called Reg, running toward Big Tree. "Look what my dad just gave me! It's my granddad's old, old compass. Granddad gave it to my dad when he was my age. Now it's mine! Whoopee!"

"That's really cool," said Burt. "I love compasses. Well, I mean I love the idea of compasses. I've never had one myself."

Reg held out a dark blue flannel bag with a drawstring at the neck. "It's in here," he said. He opened the bag and took out something round and metal. "It was one of Granddad's favorite things," said Reg. "Dad says now I am responsible enough to have it for my own."

"It looks old," said Keely, "really old."

"It is," said Reg. "Look at how the silver color has rubbed off from so much use."

"You can see the yellow metal showing through in some places," said Shawna. "It's really nice, Reg. Can you show us how it works?"

"Sure," said Reg. He opened the lid that covered the glass face. "See how the needle moves

around? The blue end always points to the Earth's magnetic north pole, which is not quite the same as the true North Pole."

"Wow!" said Shawna. "I didn't know there were two north poles!"

"Now we will never get lost," said Burt.

Reg grinned. "My dad said that a compass is not magic. You still have to keep your wits about you and use your brain too."

"Let's do something to celebrate the new compass," said Keely. "How about a hike—a long hike—an exciting hike?"

"Let's go to the Big Drop on the river," said Burt. "We've never been there by ourselves."

"That's a great idea," said Reg. "I can see which way we are going with the compass."

"Let's tell our parents," said Burt. "And we should get our backpacks and some snacks. Meet back here in half an hour?"

"I brought apples and nuts," said Keely, when they got back to Big Tree. "Let's go!"

The four friends headed off along a trail they had often walked before.

"What a great day for a walk," said Reg. "It's my first walk with my grandfather's compass. And it's our last walk before school starts on Monday." He looked at the compass face. "We have been walking northeast and now we are curving off to due east."

"What is due east?" asked Shawna.

"Just plain east," said Reg. "Not northeast, or southeast, but just plain exact eastward. See?" He showed Shawna the compass. "I turn the compass until the letter N is under the needle. Then the other letters tell us the other directions. The letter S is for south, and it's right across from north."

"Let me see," said Burt. "Oh, the E is for east, and the W is for west. I know that the sun comes up in the east and goes down in the west. And I see that northeast is halfway between north and east. This is fun!"

"We're here at the fork in the path," said Keely. "We've never gone farther than the fork without our parents. Are we up for this adventure?"

"Yes!" they all cried together. They took the right fork, the path to Big Drop.

"What does the compass say now?" asked Burt.

"The trail is now going off to the southeast. It's not very far to Big Drop."

Reg and Burt kicked little stones on the path as they went along. Keely began to whistle a tune, and the rest joined in. A dragonfly landed on Burt, and he hardly flinched.

Before long, they came to the high bank of the river. The flowing water was far below.

"Hellooooo," called Keely. Her voice called back in an echo, "Hello, hello, hello…" She reached down and picked up a small stone. She threw it high into the gorge. It dropped into the water below.

"Not like that," said Reg. He bent down and chose a stone. "Really whip it, like this." He leaned back and swung his arm as hard as he could. The rock flew from Reg's hand, and his feet flew out from under him. He fell onto his backpack.

"Are you okay?" Burt asked. He helped Reg up off the ground.

"My compass!" said Reg. "My compass slipped out of my hand. Where is it?"

Reg and Burt and Keely and Shawna looked all around. They didn't see the compass.

"I sure hope it didn't go over the edge," said Burt. "It will be really hard to find if it did."

Reg got down on his tummy and peered over the bank. "I see it!" he said. "It's on that ledge." He stretched his arm as far as he could. "I can't reach it," he said. "How can I get it back? This is awful!"

"What will your dad think if you have lost it?" said Shawna.

"Yeah," said Keely. "You are toast if you don't get it back!"

"I read something in a book once," said Burt. "It sounds silly, but it might work." He reached into his pocket and took out a stick of gum.

"Great. Gum!" said Reg. "How can you think about gum when my grandfather's compass is on that ledge?"

"The gum is part of the solution, Reg," said Burt. "It's not just for fun." He put the gum in his mouth and chewed. "I need to get the sugar out, so it will be stickier."

"And what good is sticky?" asked Reg.

Burt tilted his head down and raised his eyebrows as he looked at Reg.

"Oh!" said Reg. "Sticky! To stick to something— like something small and round and metal."

"Right," said Burt. "But first, I have to find a strong stick the right size." He picked up a stick. "Nope, not long enough."

"How about this one?" said Shawna, breaking some twigs off a branch.

"That one just might do," said Burt. "Let's try." Burt took the gum out of his mouth and stuck it on the end of the stick. "Ready," he said.

Reg lay down again at the edge of the cliff. Burt handed him the stick. "Easy now," he said. "Not too fast."

Reg lowered the stick toward the compass. The sticky gum squashed onto the metal cover. Reg pulled the stick up with a jerk, and the compass fell back onto the ledge.

"No, no," said Keely. "Slowly!"

Reg tried again. This time, he lifted the compass slowly and carefully, until he could grab it. "I have it!" he said.

"Good!" said Burt. "I thought it would work."

"I thought my heart was going to pop with the excitement," said Shawna.

"Well, that's enough excitement for today," said Reg. "Thank goodness you kept your wits about you, Burt. You really used your brain."

"Thanks," said Burt. "Hey, Reg," he said.

"Yeah?" said Reg.

"Are you going to tell your dad about what happened to the compass?"

"Sure," said Reg, "but not today. Some day, but not today."

In the Spotlight

Keely, Reg, Shawna and Burt met at Big Tree bright and early on Saturday morning. Each was carrying a bag.

"Everybody ready?" asked Shawna. "Do we all have our costumes?"

"Oh boy," said Keely. "It's dress rehearsal for the Harvest Festival play. And I have the best part!" She spun herself in a circle. "Maybe I should be an actress when I grow up."

"I thought you were going to be an artist," said Shawna.

"Or a scientist," said Burt, "like Reg."

"Yes, those too," said Keely, "but I also think I belong on the stage."

"I like my part too," said Reg. "I love being an elm tree."

"And mine too," said Burt. "I can play dirt like nobody's business. I can hardly wait!"

"Well, let's get going," said Reg. "This rehearsal is the last time we get to practice before the big show tonight."

They headed off toward school. When they got to the bridge, they met old Mr. Webber.

"Hello, kids," he said with a cheerful gleam in his eye. "Where are you off to so early on a Saturday?"

"We are going to practice our play," said Reg.

"The performance is tonight at seven o'clock. You should come. It's about plants and harvest time."

"And I am the star," said Keely. "I play Mother Nature."

"Indeed I will come," said Mr. Webber. "But first I will plant these tulip bulbs. They just came in at the nursery."

"See you tonight," called Keely, "for my big performance."

Mr. Webber waved as he shuffled away.

"You're right on time," said Mrs. Weedly, as the four trooped into the school. "The others are all here, so put on your costumes and we will get started."

Keely was the first one out of the dressing room. "Isn't this beautiful?" she said of her long green gown. "I am the Green Lady, Mother Nature!"

"You look lovely, Keely," said Shawna. "My mom did a great job of sewing these costumes, didn't she?"

"Amazing," said Keely. "She sews so well. Look how my skirt twirls, and the leafy crown is amazing!"

"Everyone for the opening scene on stage, please," called Mrs. Weedly.

Reg took his place at the back. His arms formed upraised branches of the elm tree. Keely watched from the wings. Ten kids dressed as blades of grass lined up on stage.

"Curtain!" called Mrs. Weedly. The curtains rolled open.

The grass began to sing, swaying back and forth.

"We are the grasses
that cover the ground.
We dance when a gentle
wind blows us around.
We sing when the rain
falls down on our heads.
We sleep when the winter
snow covers our beds."

Keely knew her cue and stepped onto the stage. In a strong voice, she said, "Plant a seed and watch it sprout."

Kids dressed as seeds of many kinds ran onto the stage.

"See the tiny leaves come out," Keely continued.

The seeds extended their green arms that had been behind their backs.

Burt, dressed in a dull dirt-brown costume, said, "Soil!"

Adrian, dressed in sparkling turquoise, said, "And water!"

Shawna, in gleaming gold, said, "Warmth and light!"

Keely said,

"Help the seedling grow just right.
And if it gets just what it needs,
it grows up strong and makes
more seeds."

More kids, dressed as grown plants with flowers and seedpods, ran onto the stage and recited together:

"We are the plants. We grow in the sun.
We make lots of food for everyone."

Reg and the other trees stepped forward.

> "We are the trees.
> We grow round the glade.
> We make the air fresh
> and give cooling shade.
> We give of our bounty,
> to all that we meet.
> Sweet buds, nuts and fruits
> that our friends like to eat."

When the play was over, Mrs. Weedly said, "That was great, kids. Do it just like that tonight and you can all be proud."

Reg and Keely and Burt and Shawna changed clothes and headed home.

"Wasn't I good?" asked Keely.

"You were good," said Burt.

"Good grief," said Reg. "Can't you ever stop bragging?"

"I'm just confident," said Keely. "That's a good thing."

The four friends spent the rest of the day playing, until it was time to head back to school for the play.

They put on their costumes and waited. At last it was time for the curtain to rise. The grasses did a great job playing their part, and Keely stepped out to say her lines. The stage lights shone in her eyes, but beyond the glare, she could see faces, lots and lots of faces. She saw Mr. Webber wave.

Keely felt a lump in her very dry throat. She tried to think of her line, but she could not remember it. She began to shake, and a tear rolled down her cheek.

"Keely," whispered Sarah, one of the blades of grass. "Say your line."

Keely said nothing.

A small figure in brown crept onto the stage behind Mother Nature. "It's all right, Keely," said Burt. "You will be fine. You will be wonderful. Say 'Plant a seed.'"

In a very soft voice Keely said, "Plant a seed…"

"A little louder, Keely," whispered Burt. "Plant a seed and watch it sprout."

Keely took a deep breath and said, in a louder voice,

"Plant a seed and watch it sprout."

The seeds rushed onto the stage.

"See the tiny leaves come out."

Keely smiled.

"Soil!" said Burt with a toothy grin on his face.

"And water!" said Adrian, smiling at Keely, and then at the audience.

"Warmth and light," said Shawna.

"Help the seedling grow just right," said Keely. Her voice was loud and clear. She smiled at the audience as the plants danced onto the stage. She smiled at Mr. Webber and at her parents.

Before Keely knew it, she was finished with her part and off the stage. She watched the rest of the show. Reg played his elm tree very well. When he came off stage, he asked her, "What happened to the great actress?"

Keely hung her head. "Sorry, that was mean," said Reg. "You just got a bit of stage fright. That's all. It could happen to anyone."

"But I was so sure I could do it," said Keely. "Then I saw all those people looking at me. I just froze."

Burt came up to Keely and Reg. "You were great, Keely," he said. "After the first bit, you were amazing."

"And you were the best dirt ever," said Keely. "The best dirt and the best friend. Thank you."

"It was nothing," said Burt. "It was what anyone would do for a good friend and a great actress."

"We were all good," said Shawna. "Look! It's time for our curtain call." The four friends ran onto the stage and held hands as they took their bows.

The Hunt

It was early Saturday morning and Shawna and Burt were waiting for Keely and Reg to meet them at Big Tree. Burt was sleeping at the base of the tree, and a few golden leaves had fallen onto his head. Shawna was getting a little bored.

"That's it!" she said suddenly.

Burt woke with a start and looked at Shawna through his veil of leaves.

"What's it?" he asked her.

"I'm tired of waiting for those two," she said. "Let's go get them." Shawna took Burt's arm and pulled him onto his feet. The two friends went off toward the twins' house.

When Shawna and Burt got to the house, they saw Reg's head peeking out of Keely's bedroom window.

"Oh, no!" Reg squeaked when he saw them. His head popped out of sight. Shawna and Burt ran to the window. They saw Keely still in bed with the covers pulled up to her eyes.

"Hi," said Reg. "Sorry that we didn't meet you at Big Tree. I can't get Keely to get out of bed."

Keely started to sing a song from beneath her covers.

> "It's so cold,
> And the leaves are getting old.
> I want sun,
> So I can swim and have some fun."

Reg rolled his eyes. "She's been singing that all morning," he said to Shawna.

"I love when it starts to get colder and the leaves start to change colors," said Burt. "It is fun to stay in your cozy bed."

"We've been swimming all summer, Keely," said Shawna. "Just because it's getting cold doesn't mean that we can't still have fun."

"So what should we do for fun, then?" asked Reg.

"I know!" said Burt. "We can go for a bug hunt! You love those, Keely."

"No, Burt," said Keely. "The bugs are getting ready for winter. We can't bother them. See, autumn ruins everything!"

"If we can't go on a bug hunt, maybe we can go on a treasure hunt!" said Shawna.

"That does sound exciting," agreed Keely. "But we don't have a treasure map. Where could we find one?"

"I think that people hide treasure maps where no one will find them," said Reg. "We should look in our attic!"

Shawna and Burt went inside while Keely got dressed. The four friends climbed the steep staircase that led to the attic.

"I haven't been up here for years," said Reg. "I wonder what we'll find."

"Just a bunch of old dust," said Keely.

Burt wandered over to a corner and sat down. He started to doze off. "Hey! Look what Burt found!" said Shawna. "Maybe we don't need a map to find the treasure!"

Burt woke up and looked around. "What did I find?" he asked.

"You're sitting on a treasure chest!" said Shawna. Burt stood up and looked at the old wooden chest that he had been sitting on.

Reg opened the chest, and all of the friends peered inside. Burt took out an old rope that was tied in interesting knots. Shawna found a green cap and put it on Reg's head. Keely took out a metal canteen and pretended to drink from it.

Reg pulled out a piece of yellow paper that was folded up at the bottom of the chest. "Wow!" he said when he had unfolded it. "I think I found something for our treasure hunt!" He held the paper out for his friends to see. At the top of the page, in big letters, it said "THE HUNT."

The four friends ran down the stairs and went to ask the twins' dad if he knew anything about the

paper. They found him in a big soft chair, reading a book. When he saw the paper, he smiled. "Well, it looks like you four have found my old Tree Scout chest," he said. "That is the list from a big scavenger hunt we had. If I remember correctly, I did very well in it."

"A scavenger hunt!" said Reg. "We could do that today!"

Burt looked confused. "What's a scavenger hunt?" he asked.

"It's a special kind of hunt. We each have to try to find all of the things that are on this list!" said Shawna.

The four friends ran into the kitchen and sat down to examine the paper. There were twelve items on the list. "Some of these look hard," said Burt. "How are we supposed to find a horse?"

"Scavenger hunts are supposed to be hard," said Shawna, "or else everyone would win." The friends made four copies of the list. They decided to gather items for the rest of the afternoon. Then they would meet at Big Tree before dinner to see who had found the most.

Keely went off into the woods to look for her first item. She gave a bad look to a leaf that fell to the ground in front of her. She sang to herself as she walked.

"Scavenge, scavenge, in the woods.
Scavenge, scavenge, for the goods."

By the end of the afternoon, Keely was very excited about everything that she had found. Out of twelve items, she had found ten. She skipped to Big Tree with a pillowcase filled with her treasures. Reg, Shawna and Burt were already there.

"Let the judging begin!" she said. "I got ten items, so I'm sure that I'm the winner."

"I found ten items too!" said Shawna.

"So did I!" said Reg.

"I did have ten items, but I ate most of one," said Burt.

"So how are we going to decide who won?" asked Shawna.

"I think we should look at everybody's items and decide who got the best ones," said Keely. She dumped the contents of her pillowcase onto the top of the big stump.

"We were supposed to find something that is fluffy, so I brought my pillow," said Burt. He looked like he wanted to put his head on it and go to sleep.

"I brought my fluffy sweater," said Shawna.

"I found this fluffy cotton ball in the bathroom," said Reg, while he looked at Keely's selection of items. "But it doesn't look like you found anything fluffy, Keely."

"Really?" Keely said. "What do you think this is?" She held up a light-green pod shaped like a pinecone.

"I guess it's kind of soft, but I wouldn't call it fluffy," said Burt.

Then Keely opened up the pod and showed her friends the silky seeds inside. She took a few out and let them fly away on the breeze. "It's a milkweed seedpod," she said. "Look how fluffy the seeds are."

"That's really neat, Keely," said Burt. "I bet nobody found a horse, though."

"I brought this toy horse from home," said Reg.

"I found a sawhorse in my garage, and I drew a picture of it," said Shawna, holding up the picture.

"Wait until you see my horse," said Keely. She held up something that was small, brown and shiny.

"That looks like a chestnut," said Shawna.

"You're right!" said Keely. "It's a horse chestnut from a horse chestnut tree!"

"I bet we all found something that has three colors on it," said Shawna. "I have my little sister's rattle."

"I brought my kite," said Reg.

"I found my favorite bouncy ball," said Burt.

"Look at this leaf I found!" said Keely. "It has red, yellow and green on it! Isn't it pretty?"

"You know, Keely, you found a lot of neat autumn stuff," said Reg. "I thought you didn't like it when it started getting cold."

"I guess I was too busy missing summer to remember how great fall is," said Keely. "Now I can't wait until all the leaves fall so that I can crunch through them." She started to sing and skip around Big Tree.

> "Through the leaves I'll
> crunch, crunch, crunch.
> While on the apples I'll
> munch, munch, munch."

The four friends finished comparing their scavenger hunt items. No two items were the same. "Wow," said Shawna. "It looks like we all won after all. Look at all of our treasures."

"We should do another treasure hunt when winter comes," said Keely.

Jumps Shmumps

Keely, Reg, Shawna and Burt were sitting under a tall oak tree beside the schoolhouse. It was a cold Friday in late autumn. They were all bundled up in scarves, hats and mittens.

"Wow, I can't believe that it's almost time for the Nutfest vacation," said Burt. "I can't wait to eat all of those pies and tarts and cakes!"

"I'm excited too," said Keely. "I like it when we get a break from school. It's almost like summer, except for the snow, of course."

"That's what I'm looking forward to," said Shawna. "I love the snow! I love to build forts and have snowball fights."

"You're forgetting the best thing about snow," said Reg. "Sledding! I can't wait to get out my Flying Fish again!"

A fat snowflake landed right on Burt's nose.

"Hey!" said Shawna. "The first snowflake of winter! Maybe it heard us talking about it and decided to come visit."

All of the friends ran to the middle of the field to watch the swirling snow as it got heavier and heavier.

Keely held out her arm for her friends to see. "Look at the beautiful flakes!" she said. "You can see the patterns perfectly against my dark blue sweater."

"They look like mini spider webs," said Burt, wrinkling his nose.

"I think that your sweater looks like the night sky filled with stars," said Shawna.

Mrs. Brown stuck her head out the door of the schoolhouse. "Come in from recess before you all look like snow monsters!" she called.

For the rest of the afternoon, Keely's mind wandered, even though Mrs. Brown was teaching them about the life cycle of frogs. Keely kept looking out the window at the falling snow. It was quickly covering the schoolyard. As she watched, she hummed a little bit and sang a song in her head.

Who would want to go a-frogganing,
When we all could be tobogganing?

At last, Mrs. Brown released the students. Keely, Reg, Shawna and Burt ran outside. They found a thick layer of fluffy white snow.

"Everything looks so different!" said Shawna.

"It's like the whole world changed in one afternoon!" said Keely.

"If it keeps snowing, we can go sledding tomorrow," said Reg. "Let's all meet at Mole Hill in the morning."

As soon as Keely and Reg got home, Reg ran out to the shed to find his Flying Fish. He saw it shining at the back of the shed. He dragged it past the garden hose and the tomato stakes. He smiled at the sled's comfy black seat, wide silver runners and gleaming steering wheel.

"I don't know why you need that thing," said Keely as she walked out the back door. "What's wrong with Dad's old toboggan? We can all ride it at the same time!"

"That's true," said Reg, "but you can't steer a toboggan very well, and it would break if you tried to take it off a jump."

"Jumps, shmumps," said Keely as she pulled a big wooden toboggan out of the shed. She brushed some dust off of the long red seat cushion. She untangled the red and white rope tied to the front.

Reg sat on his Flying Fish under a big pine tree. He imagined that he was flying off jumps. Keely sat down on the toboggan beside Reg. She sang him a song.

"Oh, Reggy sitting on your Fish,
as all around you snowflakes swish.
You really do make such a fuss.
Why can't you just toboggan with us?"

Reg rolled his eyes at Keely and shook his snowy head. They sat on their sleds until their mother called them in for dinner.

The next morning, Keely and Reg put on their snowsuits and headed toward Mole Hill. Reg ran ahead with the Flying Fish. Keely followed, pulling the toboggan behind her. She had loaded it with dry mittens, a thermos of hot chocolate and a bundle of fig muffins.

Shawna was already at Mole Hill. She was sitting between two fresh snow angels. "Look at all of this snow!" she said. "Isn't it terrific?"

"Stupendous!" said Keely.

"I'm going to build a big jump for the Flying Fish," said Reg. He ran up the hill.

Keely and Shawna unloaded the toboggan and shared a muffin. "You'd better mark that bump with something so that the rest of us don't hit it by mistake," Keely called to Reg.

Reg worked on his jump. Keely and Shawna tobogganed down the hill three times. Just as the jump was finished, Burt arrived at Mole Hill looking sleepy.

"Hey, Burt!" Reg called. "Watch this!"

Reg ran up the hill with his Flying Fish. He sat down on his sled. He did not notice that Keely and Shawna were about to slide down the hill too. Reg pushed off and zoomed down the hill.

"Yippee!" yelled Keely as she and Shawna sped down Mole Hill on the toboggan.

"Yahoo!" yelled Reg as he flew along on top of the snow.

Reg didn't see Keely and Shawna coming until he was almost at his new jump. They were heading straight for his landing spot!

"Look out!" Reg yelled. He leaped off of his sled in midair and landed with a thud in the soft snow. The Flying Fish shot off to the side and hit a thick pine tree.

Keely and Shawna came to a stop nearby.

"Reg!" Keely shouted. "Are you okay?" When Reg looked up he had snow all over his face. He tested his arms and legs to make sure that they still worked.

"I think so," he answered.

"It doesn't look like your Flying Fish is okay, though," said Burt. He was holding a broken sled runner in one hand and a half-eaten muffin in the other.

"Oh, no! My sled!" cried Reg. "What am I going to do now?"

"I'm really sorry about your sled, Reg," said Shawna.

"Yeah, thanks for not landing on us," said Keely. "Come on. We can all go down the hill on the toboggan."

"No," said Reg in a sad voice. "If I can't go off jumps on my Fish, I don't want to sled anymore. Maybe I won't ever go sledding again." Reg walked over to his broken sled and nudged it with his foot. He sat down in the snow beside it and sighed.

Reg spent the rest of the morning playing with a little pinecone that he found in the snow. He built a tiny jump for it and made it do flips and spins in the air. He could hear his friends laughing and pretended that they were a cheering crowd.

When it was almost time to go home for lunch, Keely walked over to Reg with two cups of hot chocolate.

"You know," said Keely between sips. "We are having a lot of fun, but I sure wish we could go down the hill faster." Keely paused to blow on her hot chocolate.

"One way to make the toboggan go faster is to put more weight on it," said Reg.

"Oh, yeah, I forgot about that," said Keely. "But what are we going to weigh it down with?"

Reg thought for a minute. "I guess I could sled with you for a while if you really need my help," he said.

"I was hoping you'd say that!" said Keely.

The twins ran to the top of the hill where Burt and Shawna were waiting for them. Keely, Burt and Shawna took their places on the toboggan, but Reg didn't get on.

"Leave room for me!" Reg said. He grabbed Burt's shoulders and started to push. He ran beside the toboggan and jumped on the back at the last minute. The toboggan flew down the hill faster than ever. When they slid to a stop at the bottom of the hill, the four friends fell into the snow, laughing.

"That was a great ride!" said Reg. "Let's come back this afternoon for more tobogganing."

While Keely and Shawna finished off the hot chocolate, Burt walked over to pick up Reg's broken sled. "I'm pretty sure that my dad can fix your

Fish," he said after looking at the runner. "Maybe then we can take turns going off your jump, if you show us how."

Reg grinned. "I like that idea!"

"I want to go first!" said Keely.

Snow Day

Keely pulled back the curtains and looked out at the morning. "Sheesharooney!" she said. "Look at all that snow!"

She went in Reg's room and shook him awake. "Reg! Wake up! There's so much snow on the ground! I'll bet we'll have a snow day!" She did a little dance. "No school today, no school today," she sang.

"Well, you are right about that," said Reg, "because it's Saturday. You woke me up early on a Saturday, and I was having a great dream."

"What was it about?" Keely asked. "Monsters? Big fierce monsters?"

"How did you know?" said Reg. "It was about something big and fierce. It was about dragons— big, scaly, fire-breathing dragons."

"What were they doing?" Keely asked.

"Nothing all that scary," said Reg. "They were sleeping and hiding and being very quiet. They did have smoke coming out of their noses as they slept."

"You have weird dreams, Reg," said Keely. She yanked off his covers. "Now, enough jibber-jabber. Let's get out in that snow!"

Mother poked her head into the room. "Hot oatmeal with currants is being served in the kitchen, if you two care to join us for breakfast."

"Just what I need to fortify me for the cold," said Keely. She dashed past her mother.

"Fortify!" said Reg. "My sister must eat dictionaries for supper!" His mother laughed.

Keely and Reg finished eating. They pulled on their snowsuits. "Let me at it!" said Reg.

Keely grabbed two handfuls of snow and smacked them together. "Perfect packing snow," she said. "It's just right for building something. What shall we make?"

"You're right," said Reg. He molded snow into

a snowball and tossed it at Keely. "It is perfect!" He ran for cover as Keely brushed the snow off her face and grabbed for more. Reg jumped behind a tree, and the snowball crashed into the trunk. "Missed me!" he yelled.

Keely threw a second snowball. It knocked Reg's hat off. "Cold!" he shrieked. "You got snow in my ears! Truce! Peace! No more. It's time to build now."

"What are you going to build?" said Keely.

"Not telling. I am going to build something spectacular!"

"And you say I use big words!" said Keely. "Well then, I am going to build something stupendous!"

"Okay," said Reg. "We'll see who builds the best thing out of snow. I'm going behind those trees to build mine because it's a secret. Don't look!"

"I'll be too busy making my own masterpiece to worry about yours. You don't look at mine!"

"You're on," said Reg. "I'll call you when my winner is finished."

"You mean my winner!" said Keely.

Reg headed off to a group of cedar trees. "No peeking!"

"As if I am even curious," said Keely. "Hhumph!" Keely scooped two huge handfuls of snow and packed it into a big snowball. Then she rolled it along the ground. As she rolled it, the ball picked up more and more snow. It grew bigger and bigger. She parked it and began another ball. When it was done, she placed it beside the first and made a third, this one a bit smaller. Her chain of snowballs grew as she added more and more. Then on the largest ball, she placed a smaller ball with a part sticking out.

"Looking good," Keely said to the snow creature. "Your snout is very nice."

Keely picked two shriveled crab apples from the crab apple tree. She stuck them into the creature's head for eyes. She molded two large ears sticking up and added some sticks for fangs. "Awesome!" she said. "But something is missing. She needs arms." Keely found some branches. She stuck them into the largest ball.

She began to sing.

"She's almost right.
She's a beautiful sight.
She's almost right—
But not quite."

Keely picked up more snow. "I know what she needs," she said. On top of each ball, behind the head, she molded a scale sticking up. "That was it," said Keely. "She is just right now."

Reg stepped from behind the cedars. "You can come see my creation, now," he said. "You won't believe how great it..." Reg stopped and stared at Keely's creature. "It's a...a..."

"It's a dragon, silly. Isn't she a beauty? I win, of course."

"It is good," said Reg. "Really good. I like the little fins on the back. But now you have to come and see what I made. You won't believe it!"

The two went past the stand of cedars. Keely's mouth opened when she saw the tall figure of a dragon standing against the trunk of a tree. "I climbed the tree to add the high parts," said Reg. "It was hard work."

"I'll bet it was," said Keely. "That is one good dragon—as good as mine, almost. I like the pinecones on the tail. And what is that red in the mouth?"

"Red berries! Nice touch, isn't it? It looks like fire, sort of, doesn't it?"

"Too bad we built them where they can't see each other," said Keely. "They would get along well."

"Maybe after we leave, they will creep around and get together," said Reg.

"Or go flying together," said Keely. "We can come back later and see if they are any closer."

"I don't think they will move until nighttime," said Reg. "Aren't dragons night creatures?"

"You're right," said Keely. "Maybe we will both dream of dragons tonight and find them together tomorrow."

"What should we do now?" said Reg. "Let's get the others and see if the pond ice is ready for skating."

"Good call, Reg," said Keely. "I feel like winning a race today!"

Award-winning author **Jo Ellen Bogart** has written many popular picturebooks and non-fiction books for children. She loves animals and has had many unusual pets over the years, including, at the moment, a frog that she got as a tadpole twenty-three years ago. She lives in Guelph, Ontario. Jo Ellen's daughter and co-author, **Jill Bogart**, is an art history student and writer. She lives with her husband and son in Pittsburgh, Pennsylvania.

Orca Echoes